Flames of a Rose

Lorna Joy Knox nee Ramsamugh

PublishAmerica
Baltimore

First printing

ISBN: 1-4137-4341-2
PUBLISHED BY
PUBLISHAMERICA, LLLP.
www.publishamerica.com
Baltimore

Printed in the United States of America

To my loving husband, Noel, for his undying devotion.

To my three beloved children; Stacey-Ann, Joshua and my eldest, Andrei, for their lifetime love and support.

To all my family.
Thank you.

Acknowledgements

My poem entitled 'My Rose' was entered as a semi-finalist in the International Poetry Competition and was accepted for publication in an anthology titled *Letters from the Soul* ISBN: 0-7951-5160-8 United States Library of Congress (coffee table edition—August 13, 2002).

A second poem entitled 'My Love' was entered as a semi-finalist in the International Poetry Competition-accepted for publication in an anthology titled *Patterns of Life* ISBN: 0-7951-5239-6 United States Library of Congress (coffee table edition—January 10, 2003).

Two Tales of Mystery, a childrens' book ISBN 1-4137-5308-6 published by PUBLISHAMERICA, LLLP United States of America

A Feathered Loss

Why sit and wait in
My lonely shell,
set among the roses
amidst the holy sun
sparking its rays of light
on me in the deep, deep fields?

Should I wait for my moon to glow
as I peep my round eyes
bursting with fervour,
yet white from darkness as
the rainbow of light
warms my skin?

How many travels should I make
within my shell,
curled up for eternity?
It seems as lonely as the night
as single as the day as whirlwind grasps
Taking me through musical motions
as rough as its eye,
back to my gentle spot
set among the roses.

Should there be many more days left
as I wait,
The weeks to appear
Then months, only enormous
years now to carry my life
In one lonely shell,
sailing through that vacuum
of space, petals holding me?
Will my tears ever fall
dried from patience,
emotions abundant,
withheld in one lonely heart,
fed by thoughts
dreams, love beseeching
echoing among the mountains
shaking my lonely shell,
yet it leaves,
for my heart to bleed,
once more?

Would love ever be my tether
while I dream endlessly,
as I begin to travel to a new home
still sealed in my lonely shell?

My Rose

What has become of thee,
You…always full of glee?
Is it something that I have done
to make you, oh so woesome?

Speak my dear, I need to know
what hurts you so?
Now, I see you cry, pray…tell me why?

My heart is full of love,
you gentle little dove.
For you…only you…
I tell you, it is true!

You shine with beauty.
I am…forever at your duty.
What shall I do
to comfort you?

My beautiful rose…
those slender toes,
that creamy, chocolate skin.
My dear…I am forever
at your whim.

Heaven

His vision appears before me,
flashing in the sky, arms pulling, to set me free.

His eyes penetrate me,
he sees the worries that cause me to bereave.

His voice strong and firm, telling me,
his support is truly long-term.

My tears he sees,
my footsteps printed by the old oak trees.
He lifts me high, carries me wide across the sea,
the mountain, the rivers, shows me his beautiful feat,
his special place, all designed for me.

He sets me by his side,
His archangels circle me wide.
The white-scented flowers sweeten the air,
the lions and bears free and purring, from love and care.

His protective hands set me down, among the daises,
by the river to relax at last.
Finally, to forget my miserable past.

Love in the Park

Closed hands
we walk in the park
raindrops falling down,
one by one.
The pigeons fly off
in their flock,
flowers in their glory surround.

The silence of our touch, sweet hushed tones,
endearing thoughts,
kisses and hugs,
As we walk through this quiet place so cool,
so blue,
we, in love.

Our palms never untwined
Sweet strong love in this gardenious cove.
more wet kisses, all over my face,
two hearts,
gentle endearing
in one place.

Momentary kisses, so wet and many,
this garden of love in its magnetic beauty,
for love, a beautiful charm.

My Cry

I cry out to thee,
tears streaming down my face.
I need thee in my place,
to feel my pain,
to hold me, cuddle me.

I cry for thee,
you pretend not to see,
that mine heart doth hurt,
mine soul doth bleed,
for you, you alone.

You now look into mine eyes,
probing to see beyond.
Thine hands so warm, so strong.

You now want to love me,
build thy temple around mine soul,
to never leave me,
to always love me,
blended and bonded, forever
You and I, now bleedeth as one.

Lonely Heart

Ripped from its warm home
placed out at sea.
Left to search and roam,
as lonely as can be.

Waves bobbing up and down,
to carry this heart through.
Strangled by the sea,
overgrown,
now cold, cold and blue.

The ship passes by the tide,
bouncing this heart against its side.
Afflicting some hurt,
leaking blood, a little spurt.

This heart, it searches for a new home,
waiting, hoping for some good atone.
It cries out so weak,
a voice so soft, tender and meek.

No one appears to hear,
God Bless! It's too much to bear!
Take me from this pain,
I have lost all, all my flame.

Moonlight glazes across the sea,
two lonely hands reach out for me.
So far a distance to this great shore,
to finally find love, someone to adore.

This heart, no more to bleed,
its side, now well sealed.
These hands to nurture me,
given a new home, forever love, to be.
This lonely heart, its love inflamed,
its longing cries, eternally embraced.

Undying Love

I look into thine eyes
so deep and glazed.
glowing, like a sun blazed.

I see thy nose,
Hooked in pose
flaring in warmth
friendly, pulling me in close.

Thy sweet lips
won't leave me be,
thine hands so warm,
blazing with charm.

You see me.
You touch me.
You love me.
Always, meant to be.

The Golden Ring, of Love

To hold mine hand,
to place on mine finger,
that beautiful wedding band.

To sayeth thy love for me
to feel thy pain and agony,
mine love to do without,
you would not be.

Mine soul eternal is for thee
and no other, my love.
Take me now as I am
as you want me, here.

I do pray for us both
to live beyond our love,
together, together.

Pray, take me now.
For thine love, mine heart is weak.
I love thee.

In Love Forever

His eyes roam over me
lazy and hungry.
Twinkles in his eyes
seeing me, looking so sultry.

He stirs with unease
my body his big tease.
Low moans in his throat,
looking so weak, as if afloat.

Firm hands grasp me now
caressing so gentle, he knows how,
it is too much to bear.
In my mind, I see it so clear.

His breath so warm
soft whispers, full of charm.
Slow wet kisses
every inch, he never misses.

Strong hands stroke my face,
he makes me feel like precious lace.
Squeezes my arms pulling me near,
hungry kisses, sending me asteer.
I am to him, his ever-loving dear
our life now, forever clear.

Human Sacrifice

To take me as a sacrifice
locked in that cage screaming out
in fiery rage,
for you know not what you do to me,
To enslave me
place me in this vicious bondage?

To choose me as a sacrilege,
as the human flesh to feed on your hungry bellies,
groaning like beasts,
to gouge mine eyes with fiery wood, to carry me around
that whirlpool of thy envious eyes
to scrape, to maim me?

To feel saliva drool from thy mouths
those hands grabbing, tearing, gnawing,
ripping my soul into a thousand pieces
to be eaten raw, like a beast of evil.

Dreams

Dreams, of a garden of beautiful flowers,
as a single rose, one sparkling magnet of beauty,
watered every day, petted and stroked
treated like a queen, soft and pure
cared to shine, the whole outdoors.

Dreams, as that one rose in a garden,
to see the talking hands, the watering can,
feel the embrace of the sun,
the cool of the wind, the softness of the rain
bathing my soft petals, keeping me vain.

Dreams, as the only rose in a garden
the queen above the rest,
to rule divine and pure, give them all the allure
of my simple petals, my stalk, my stem,
invigorate in my beauty,
to share it, only with them.

Dreams, as the queen of this garden
bright and exploding, to beckon the faithful hands,
to sprinkle me, to treat my friends,
even under the dark knighted lamps.

I am their queen in this luscious garden
so mellow and complete.
They only need to stick with me,
to be gifted treated sweet.

Honeysuckle, daffodil, marigold, my strong bond with you,
and you others, I am your queen, I do love you too.

Spirit

The spirit was bright and laughing,
playing games, children in a circle.
Eyes twinkling like the starry nights.
Wild, like the blazing fire
crackling, from the wood.

The spirit was strong and bold
fearless and cheerful,
Opening the windows to see the sun
so glazed and shining, warm and full.

The spirit crept underneath that
wide thick rug, hiding from the eyes,
black piercing eyes from every corner,
glaring viciously, tearing apart.

The spirit could no longer stand
the slice of that sharp blade.
The spirit lays down, soul drained weaker
weaker, choking in froth, frail as a wilted leaf.

The spirit looks at the grave open wide
freshly dug, coffin new and shining.
The spirit keepers gather around, sombre and down
with that black book, its words jumping out,
putting it aground.

The spirit is now gone, the spirit has died.
Silence, is very strong.
The sun shines no more,
the fire is out, the stars all vanished.

Oh angelic spirit, where have you gone?
Come back; bring your soul, if you can.
Are you really gone?

This Artist

This brush paints on canvas
the world so grey,
The clouds dotted in the sky,
mountains overlapping
the calm blue sea,
Its waves gently lulling ashore,
by the reef,
by the sand.
Seagulls encircle.

This brush paints on canvas
the ship out at sea,
light buoy bobbing out deep,
the sun going down
bright orange.
One star forms in the sky,
the waves rush madly ashore
climbing over the reefs.

This brush paints on canvas
the sun rising.
This morning awakening
that large flock of white birds
zooming across the calm blue sea.
Ship now at shore, boasting its beauty,
pulling out its large haul of fish.
ruling the sea, triumphant in feat.

This brush paints on canvas,
a picture every day,
each time the scenery, gives way.
it never tires,
it never aches,
to keep this wondrous picture
in its true place.

Lonely…in Pain

She sits cross-legged, hands on her knees,
darkness caves in, as black as the night, hard and mean.
Not one single light, those eyes to see,
grasping so tight, trapped, no more free.

Tears like a slow-moving river, pour out from her eyes,
her body bent down, blinding her sight,
Her tiny body racking from side to side,
loud sobbing cries,
echoing, echoing, straight through the skies.

Strong sharp pain, like a bolt of lightning,
pierces through that lonely heart, forever fighting,
to believe, to have some hope in her life,
to wish an angel would have ended the strife.

The wind whistles eerily through the windowpane
so tight.
The sky so bright, yet as dark as the night.
Her face now stained with tears, long straggly hair
blowing so light.
Still she looks around,
the darkness is still,
it surrounds with all its might.

Endless, endless pain to rack her brain.
Cries, more cries, what will ever end this vicious chain?

Moonglow

Flurries of feathers
blow with the wind,
as I walk slowly through the dusky evening.

The sky like huge puffs of smoke
around the dark mountains,
no sign of life.

Only the dark grey owl up
in the tree I see,
perched on the branch so mysteriously.

Slowly, as I walk along,
the slow-moving wind pushes me on,
flurries of feathers beseech to me,
to carry me.

The half-moon is out now, the air so mystical
the night moves on, as I tread along
the winding road, to watch
sparking stars flicker, send magnets
of light to my body.

Moon now full, night is still, still.
The night reaches for me, enfolds me,
entwines me, to claim me.
This one, mystical night.
The night, only for me.

Dark Silent Cries

Alone in the dark, a huge burden bearing down on me,
like tons of steel strapped to my bones giving me no free.
My brain conjured of thoughts, scattered thoughts
of what to do to keep my mind anew.

Standing in solid darkness, not one sole light
to keep me from this fright that faces me every day,
no one to help me from this pain, to stop this vicious stain.
No hand to hold, no secure, everything gone far, far away.

Walking so light as if on thin air, my spirit begs for the good clear,
to stop my stress, keep me from fear.
They do me wrong, for so long,
I have grown tired, so weak, and no more strong.

They walk around me like darkened shadows,
no friends to me.
My life so lonely, where else can I be?
Reckless hands hit me so hard, like a thousand rocks
hurling mad, only for me.

This life is no more for me; the space is too filled,
my smiles are masks of darkness.
This strong gait is really weak, no more a big billed.
Raindrops fall down on me like blood of madness,
no hope, no love, just nothing, its sadness.

Crying is now the norm, more like a storm.
This evil bites too hard, like a vampire
eager for a fit form.
My eyes have grown as white as snow,
my lips are now cracked,
my lips now plastic,
my heart is ripped,
I am, no more.
I am, now still.

Shining Knight

Smile for me, right now
Deep into mine eyes.
Smile for me, look now,
I see thine face so beautiful,
it is you I love.

Touch mine face, right now,
feel mine skin,
touch me now, feel me.
I see thine hand, so strong.
it is you to love.

Hold mine hand, right now,
so warm and soft,
feel mine hand, so soft.
I see thyself so brave.
It is you, to love.

Thine armour so grand,
my love,
The palace awaiteth,
the king's stand.

You are my knight, in love.

Roses in Bed

One bounteous bed of roses,
red, white and pink.
Sweet cotton nightgown
on this soft creamy skin,
to feel the luxurious smell
of petals so soft,
to caress me gently.
in sweet, invigorating comfort.

To toss and turn,
with pleasureous delight.
This beautiful creation,
it is a heavenly sight.
Soft burning candle so light,
to warm me more,
my passions to fight.

Hair around my shoulder
in gentle perfume,
silky and shining, my head in tuned
to the glorious moments,
which I await, to anticipate
only to wait, wait.

The candle is out,
on soft feathery down
I lay abound,
unsoothing passion,
from this bed of soft,
soft roses.

Infinity

In the hills,
far beyond the mountains,
the old grand house in its lavish kingdom,
lawns with giant water fountains.

To see, summer breezes wave the golden grass,
to dance among fresh herbs, jasmine in such golden class.
To feel, the air of the night in its gentle might.

The warmth of this glorious beam of moonlight
sparkling so bright,
flowery petals dance through the night
golden sheaves of corn in that wide space,
a beautiful sight.

A wondrous beauty in this life,
to live forever, in death.
to feel this glory, so in depth
to float in this path, infinite kingdom.

Gentle wind to lift this soul up high,
in this definite kingdom,
around the world, back to this place,
this wondrous, wondrous euphoria!

Peace

Butterflies flutter all around me
Bright, pretty colours.
The sun shines so warm,
glowing all around me.

Those birds in the sky, so white
look down on me
they speak to me,
comfort me.

The grass so green,
its shade so bright,
envelops me.

The pond is my mirror,
so clear
giving me my image
it paints me, claims me.

These tall trees
hover above me.
They protect me, guard me
they keep me safe.

There is,
no darkness.
Only light,
dazzling, beautiful rays of light.
Peaceful,
this is heaven.

Soul

The soul mortal, yet immortal
to die so quickly, to live so long.

The soul envelopes the warm earth, the spirit to live on,
to die so hard, to live so strong.

The soul to roam the earth, to live a life of peace,
new hope, new friends, no more to grieve.

The soul is free, free to be true.
No more injury, pure, wholesome ado.

The soul survives in wintry storms, never calmed.
No need to worry, this soul is totally embalmed.

This soul lives forever.
Forever,
forever.—
—

Blind

Mine eyes are blank,
dried.
Not one, tear to fall.
Itching, itching
emotionless, tearless, painless
forcing, forcing, not one…
Single tear to fall.

Beyond

Life across the seas
over the oceans
past the ships,
the isles.

Across mountain slopes
trees and roads,
life, beyond.

Memories

Memories of cheerful times
as cheerful as the sunny days
the sparkling sun glowing from the sky,
lush trees branching out wide
smiles as happy as sweet singing melodies.

Memories of happy days
white sandy beaches to laze,
sand as white as snow,
water as pure as gold,
Towels as bright as the rainbow.
Red peppered shrimps, peanuts
spritzy sprites,
to lap in this sweetest nature
for so many days and nights.

Memories of smiling children
laughter like echoes through the ocean
to watch them so merry
eating juicy strawberries, bright red cherries
shining through the rising waves.
To this beautiful luxury, we nourish like slaves.

Memories of love,
God sent angels from up above,
one happy family, as free as the wind
a small round circle as magical as the sun
to keep us together
love forever, having fun.

Music

Musical bells so sweet in my ear
how many times to hear this beautiful cheer!
It sounds to me, like singing doves
a small orchestra and a whole lot of loves.

Soft sweet melodies
through the trumpet of sounds
hummings of a violin,
sweet music on its rounds.

Guitar strings strum, one by one
rippling tunes to sing me along.

My ears begin to tinkle
my eyes begin to shine,
with a little winkle.
My lips curve in smile to the tune
my mind is heaven, smiling with the moon!

Beautiful Mind

Flowers in my mind
springing about, fully unwind.
Smiling so bright
beautiful, beautiful rays of light.

White doves encircle my head
a nice white halo, lulling me to bed.
Their feathers as white as snow
tiny eyes so warm, gifted from head to toe.

Wings outspread, they carry me along,
to rest in sleep, to keep me strong.
Tender soft feathers caress my skin,
to send me off, calm slumber to begin.

The morning awakens to warm sunlight,
fluttering butterflies to bring me delight.
Flittering before my eyes, in my mind,
to wake up, they treat me so kind.

My mind so light and free,
my true friends to stay with me.
Always close by my head,
to enter, keep me in good stead.

This One Man

He stands alone,
one man to stride this world,
firm in faith, he sees glory ahead
heading straight for that point, in full stead,
never to shed one single tear
holds all his pain, without a fear.

He stands so strong
this man, sure to carry on
to achieve in life without a strife,
squashes his enemies, without a knife,
to turn his head, without the flicker of an eye,
to keep his life.

He loves so warm
though sharp and gruff, but with a gentle calm,
underneath that stead is one warm soul
to sacrifice his life, to keep his family whole.

This one man
so rough, loves with a passion so inflamed,
no matter what, that hand never leaves
always there, never to be blamed,
but to love, to stay together
love, without vain.

Evil

Evil lurks behind the
walls,
curtains,
on the street,
everywhere, it's there to be.

Witchery displayed in
smiles,
guiles,
innumerable sin.

Coats of all colours,
watch,
glare,
deep glowing penetrating eyes
bursting from the sleeves
on constant guard.
Fear of,
missing the next move
not being a part of the next scene
gory to the details,
wrenched from behind
legs twisted like a rope
bent like a ball
head severed
Spurts of blood splattered…
grinded and churned
to a frazzle of dust
left, to rot
to blow in the wind,
to disappear, finally…out of the way.

Stagnate

The world has stopped
dead in its tracks,
for me.
The sun rises no more
stuck below the mountains,
to me.
The moon never glows
sky black with the stars,
on me.
How many rivers
to drown the sorrows
of my deepest horrors.
Why me?

Hidden Love

Our eyes met
on that first day,
my lips sealed
nothing to say.

You give to me
so much,
to let me be free
to see thy true face
to know you are a good pace.

You'd never know
how much I need you so
as my eyes avert
from your alert.

The years go by
to love you so
I know now,
I'll love you,
till I die.

So near, yet so far
this distance
A big bar
Right now, the hurt so strong
Two of us to get along.

Not one word from you
I wonder what you do
The long days,
The long nights,
This strong feeling, strong fights.

I pretend not to see
As you pass by me
No words said
Only to fall in love with you,
Instead.

I love you so
You'll never know,
My love for you,
Always true.

Roses

Roses bent,
As sweet perfume
Shoots across the garden.
Sweet, sweet scents
To heighten every sense.

Roses red,
Lovers' core,
Bunch of twelve
Soft vibrant petals
To soften old harden metals.

Roses white
Innocence stored.
Pure, and holy.

The Daughter's Mirror

Horrific tale
Of the maiden made
Constant flow of music
Bloody from its core.

Given a wench's gore
Evil ogres' adore
Placed under the matting sun
To melt like mucky butter.

Insults like hurling stones
From the old irons' doors
Pitched with a devil's fork
Like an old witches' part.

Words of bitter gall
From fiery tongue
In a mound of darkness placed.
The world so nasty, so unfaced.

The Valley and the Lilies

The valley is wide and green
Lilies abound gloriously,
It is sunset with magnificent views,
The sky glistens with beauty,
It is beautiful!

Lilies, lilies all over,
So alive, yet so serene
Yet so sad…
What have become of thee my lilies?
I dare say, I wish I could take your place!

Miseries abound, heart so sad,
Pray, let me be one of you?
Bring my heart some console…
What do you worry about?

You are very lucky indeed,
No troubles no bother,
You have peace, happiness around you!
Be merry!

Your smiles make me happy, yet sad
Yes, all you beautiful lilies!
I love you…
Be at peace.

Life is good,
life is sad,
Life is full of so much misery,
So much hatred, but you lilies,
I love you.

This Beauty, in Distress

Long flowing black hair
She gets quite a stare.
Long chiselled nose
She strikes quite a pose.

Her lips full and wide
Her big round eyes abide
Behind that laughter,
Behind that smile
Yet only for a while.

Good mother of three
Those kids meant to be,
Happy and strong
A mom to help them along.

This mom, full of life,
Never in for a strife.
Happy as a lark, but sick
Watching that clock
Waiting for its next tick.

They called her a fake,
Pinning her to the stake
Accused of whining,
That heart was only pining
For love,
Of hurt, she was dying.

The final day came,
It was no more a game.
This tropical dame
Finally gained fame…in death, her last breath.

It was true,
NOW…all could see.
Finally made free,
She was free.

Tears now flow,
What a huge blow
If they had known
They never would have,
Thrown that stone
At death…at beauty

My Precious Mom

Tall, dark beauty
She smiled sweetly.
Calm, gentle soul
Wrapped in that fur stole.

Her smile so tender,
Fingers all slender.
My mom she was,
Slight, gentle buzz.

My mom was ill,
Not left with much will.
Waiting to die,
To say good-bye.

She lay on the bed.
I watched her,
Waiting for dead.
All that love,
Now taking her above.

Her eyes met mine,
I knew…she'd be fine.
Then, she was gone.
I was left to carry on.

Precious Gran

Warm and kind,
Hugs and kisses.

Tenderous spot,
From this old knot.

My old gran,
Best of the lot.

Twelve whole kids,
All now bigs.

Grandmamma hey!
You are one brave.

To knight you now,
'lighted feather.'

Sparks of light,
With all your might.

Like a strong chief,
Brave and strong.

To spoil me along
With sweets and cakes.

Take me through my mother's grief,
Grandmamma love, you are one chief!

Firelight

The match strikes,
To light that stick
Flickers of light shooting
Way, way up
Sparks of explosion to sparkle the skies,
So magnificent.

The match strikes
Yet, multicoloured haze
Across the sky, explosive blasts
To waken the night,
So fantastic.

The match strikes
Now five together, bomb blasts.
Thrilling explosion to awaken
The world, unite in one soul,
So exciting.

This match
With its envious power
To create a world, indefinite unite,
Huddled up close, to read the words.

One match for you, one match for me
One match to bring us
In strong unity.
Celebrate!

Serenity

My heart welts like a plant,
Starving of water.
My soul is bled like,
A river running dry.
It is sad, but what can I do?

I wonder, is there hope!
My body yearns for happiness,
For peace.
Is there hope still yet?

Homely, peaceful desires,
To make my life fulfilled.
Quiet life,
No strife.

Criticism abounds,
Flags renounce.
I need to relax
To get back on my tracks.

Sacrifices, love…
A lot to give.
Friendships would be good,
If only I could.

Quiet nurtures,
Quiet life,
That's what I like.
Hate this strike,
Give me back my life?

Friends

Friends of love, far and wide.
Still and silent, full of pride.

Friends of kindness love to give.
No more sorrow, hopes to live.

Friends of culture, full of fame.
Showered with gifts, treated like a dame.

Friends to treat, it is true love.
Friends to keep, lots of good cove.
Friends to take me through the cloud
To keep me standing, make me proud.
No more pain, but friendly gain.
Like a wild horse, now calm, now tame.

Me

Wide, green valleys surround
Lush green grass.
Trees grow so majestic
Tall and glorious.
Flowers bloom…
Golden primrose, marigold, wild rose!

Stream ever so quiet…
The cool breeze so light,
Mountains huge and voluptuous,
Skies all grey,
So still,
So clear.

All this glory around…me,
Me alone,
Sitting by that stream
Looking at my shadow
Dark and gloomy.

No existence.
No speech.
Just…
Me.

The Lily's Song

Assumptions are made,
Destructions follow,
This lily, she has been affected
Tears follow, day after day.
This lily, full of sorrow.

Frustrated, depressed, lonely…
Feeling like an outcast,
Sanity withheld, oh those blessed baby lilies!

Living day by day
Stifling of grief,
Smiles abounding, lots of gaiety!
This lily is happy, is she?

Cries of abundance,
Tempers flaring,
Hurting, hurting
Cries of mercy, cries for help,
This lily…she weeps.

Love is plentiful!
Hugs and kisses abound.
Screams of playing, gurgling of laughter,
This lily, she smiles.

An Artist

An artist
Most famous to me,
Pencil eternal in hand
From the tender age of three,
Paints my world of sparkling colour
No need to even see a flower.
A tireless hand to give me humour
Animations abound to have me, laughing in one long stupor.
No need to even see a video, this master of invention
He has my undivided attention.
Twelve midnight and never a fight
Scattered papers, colours, draws, with all his might.
His dream in animation, bound to bring this world
Howls of laughter, he is my long-term dedication.
This artist…world class!

My Little Gem

My little gem,
Full of twirls,
Her hair, all curls.
She sits stroking her pet's furs.

My little gem,
Ever so rare,
Each day more fair,
Loves to dress up.
Always, looking on top.

My little gem,
Her beautiful bouncing hair,
Gets a lot of stare,
My gem, so rare.

My little gem,
She knows her books.
She's no floops,
Puts out a lot of write,
Even with a lot of fight.

My little gem,
Fights,
Cries,
Smiles,
Radiates, even with her wiles!

This little gem,
Is not all beauty.
She likes a lot of duty.
So, this precious gem,
Gets all the love.
She's like an angel,
From up above.

Strength

Strength is,
This son standing tall,
Firm enough to push the wall.
Tall, dark handsome in all his princely glory,
Plushed to whip up a gigantic story.

Strength is,
The tornadoes viciously around,
This son, his feet still on the ground.
He carries that heavy weight,
Like a luggage-carrying freight.

Strength is,
All the sadness in the world,
He outwardly remains uncurled.
He carries that metal on his shoulder,
Like a tractor lifting boulder.

Strength is,
Frustrated and depressed,
He never stops to rest,
Still goes around,
Have the music asound.

Strength is,
Rain, sunshine, wintry showers,
This son still maintains his powers.
This son, he makes me proud,
I need to shout it loud.

Age from a Babe

Age from a babe
From its mother's womb it was made.

Wrapped so warm in woollen clothes,
Ten creamy-coloured fingers and toes.

One nobby little nose, tiny toothless smile
To sparkle one's heart, if not but for a while.

A perfect picture placed in the mind
One beautiful snap to frame, caught well timed.

His skin as soft as the petal of a rose
Its warm breathing, I feel it, he knows.

The precious moments go by
So heavenly, at times to see him cry.

Bundled on my shoulder, feel his tender cheek against mine,
That comforted smile, eyes twinkling so fine.

Now tall and strong, one big man,
Rippling muscles, firm sprinting legs in a dark tan.

'Twas my care for him to come thus far,
Splendid inches above me now, height no more on par.
'Twas my undying love,
Yes, 'twas wholesome loving from this good mom!

My Love

I dare say,
To have loved thee away
Send thee astray
No more a day
With thy love.

Why have thee
So far and bent,
To be mine
Thus mine alone
Gone so far?

Hath thou lovest me
My love to be,
I'd still be here
Your loving dear.

Come back my love
I need that cove,
I long for that touch,
Need you so much.

Lonely Night

Toss and turn
Underneath that sheet.
Twisted, wrapped from head to toe
Skin warm and soft,
Only to burn
From this loss of love,
Still to learn
Of this lonely pain
Reaching out in vain.

Toss and turn
Beneath the cover
Without a lover,
Still to cry
From this lonely pain
To whisper out, his name.

Toss and turn
The hours go by
Time to say good-bye
To nightful dreams
Of hopeful means.

Toss and turn
To fall asleep
In deep, deep sleep.

White Rose

This lonely white rose
As pure as silk,
Smooth against flesh
To break the senses.

Lonely as ever,
It bends in pain,
Its petals frail from
The stain of abstinence.

One lonely white rose.

The Lonely Vine

The vine on the fence, no one ever sees,
Long, entwining, for miles and miles,
Bled from hurt, weather-beaten,
Chopped at times,
Lonely, with all the passing cars,
Blaring lorries, bikes in full blast.

Its edges so sharp, fierce from cold
Pleading for care, someone to even to be bold,
No one ever stops to touch this vine,
To think it may need a soft tender mind.

Just one touch, from its rough beginning
To soften throughout its endless miles,
Into one warm relaxing vine.
One touch, it smiles.

Woes

Woes like a turbulent tide
Like waves raging, roaring in
The ocean,
Rising,
Falling,
Crashing down so viciously.

Woes like ten thousand years
Trouble on endless days,
To hurl my mind in a different era
Sailing through the space.

Woes like endless tragedy
Dead so many times
Lost among the twining vines.

Woes like evil ghosts,
Hauntings of a thousand years
Knotting of an innocent brain
To endless tears and wears.

Lover's Quarrel

What have thee to say to me now,
Latching me behind strong bars?

How dare thee put up a stripe
Build up thus terrible rife on a wife?

Can thou widen that mouth
Tell thee, isn't that enough?

Henceforth, I say
To keep that latch free,
Take thine axe,
Bring some fine meat for me.

Thou aren't so bitter
Under that stip.
Thyself, I know
Much, much fitter.

Thou art mine friend in need,
I love thee very much indeed.

Thy crusty hand
To clench mine,
To work together,
This beautiful land.

I love thee.

A Little Love

Love to me,
I need.

Love to me,
You know?

Love to me,
Somehow.

Love to me,
Right now!

Love me!

The Wintry Daze

Trees as bare as the wintry nights,
Leafless branches like ghostly sights
Trunks as firm as a thousand years
Still to stand, through all the tears.

To sway through the wintry airs
Soft smooth sways,
Behold this enchanting gaze
Surrounded by wispy fogs,
These old awesome wooden logs.

Red-bricked cottages,
As bright as day
To sit below these kingly rays
Of darkened lights
Standing,
Like guarded knights.

Trees as tall as the sky,
Invisible elves and gnomes
To make these branches good homes.
As quiet as the hushed night,
This old majestic wintry sight.

Grey Strands of Hair

One lonely road to trod
Under the watchful eye of God,
Followed through the blistering snow
One grey strand now to grow.

Hardest toil day by day
No time for frivolous play
Still, no more chores to do
Another gray strand to form anew.

Nighttime woes for the bus to roll
Patience out, quiet tempers growl
To see it finally arrive
Crowded, what a spite!
To hang on strong, pushed about
More grey strands for this old rote.

The days go by
Same old stories to make me sigh,
A change of pace, this book in hand
To give me one more,
Glorious grey strand.

River Chant

The river, slow and moving
The evening as dark as magic
Wind whistles through the air
The tall pines dance gently
From side to side
Slowly, ever so slowly.

The mountain slopes
Like darkened shadows
The sun hidden below,
Like orange rays blasting
Like bolts of light across
The river.

Glazed, moving slowly, ever so slowly,
One lonely Indian sent ashore
Death from a fight
A warrior's might.

Moccasins on his feet
Feather in his hair
Bravest heart to die
The drums beat…and beat…beat.

Out he goes,
Slowly, slowly down the river
The lilies follow, green and alive
Tall wispy reeds surround.

One match to strike,
Fiery blaze to send
One brave in that infinite place.

The evening gets darker
The pines are still,
Mountains as dark as giant ghosts.
The river still…
The wolf howls,
And howls
Through the night
One single star, so far.

One magical night
In death's fight with
One lonely Indian.

The wolf howls,
howls,
and howls.

Death at the Gallows

Why dost thou afflicteth me so sorely,
Injureth mine flesh, mine mind?

Dost thou have no mercy, to slice mine soul
With thy shadowy blade?

Why hath thee bounded me in tight chains
To drip mine blood from its every tear?

Thou art no fool mine eyes hath seen,
So why won't thou endeth this foolish damnation?

Why preparest that guillotine, while I lamenteth
Out to thee for mercy, mercy?

Why placeth mine head on that sharp block,
To feeleth that sharp wrenching of that huge axe?

Mine lamentations goeth in the air,
Thine heart so cold for this innocent dear!

Mercy!..mercy!…mercy.

Thine axe reacheth now, I knoweth in one second,
Mine pain…will be no more.

Wrath of a Babe

Dark wraps around its nape
Slavery etched from a tape
Window plight from the whitening eye
Stronged up cord
On good nature,
Abhorred.

Lash of an evil bat
On its nightly chore,
Stiff on bending branch
To tear a babe outdoor.

Babe of innocence,
Blackness of incense
To welcome a grave
For a lowly slave.

Blanket of bloody bats
A babe in gory tucks,
To die from death's cord
In insane accord.

Heartache

The pain screaming out…
The heart bleeds,
For love,
For belonging.

The mind dreams of hands entwined,
Of quiet strolls.

The body yearns for strong smooth strokes,
Like a lover's adore.

The earth shatters
With one lonely person
In need of infinite love.

The world closes.
Love has gone
To suffer no more…
In this eternal abyss.

From Dickens Estate

A challenge from
Charles Dickens Estate,
A poet's lifelong fate.

To watch red double-deckered
Buses pass by,
Abbey Street nearby.

Florists with sweet-smelling flowers
Cafés with strong aroma of coffee
Grocery shops, as sweet as sugar and candies.
Post Office for stamps and posting.

This town of Bermondsey…
As rustic as a ship's core
As fresh as the breeze from the sea
To watch the planes go by
Flashing lights from up above,
Blinking through the nights.

Southwark Park as large as can be
Like an old wintry tale,
Its many trees scattered about I see
Collar on dog, master on hand
To walk so slowly
In fresh clean air.
To see the trees all bare
An old poet's tale
In this literary place.
In this old…Charles Dickens Estate.

Thoughts

Pretty, picturesque view
Brown-bricked English cottages
Cool sunny day
The sun blinding to the eye
Puffs of cloud sailing slowly
…slowly through the sky
demanding an enchanting gaze
hypnotizing…
hypnotizing my mind in a wary daze.
Only the clouds and sun to brighten
The dark bricked buildings
Canvas and brush to beckon
Wide lens camera for this
Pretty picture…
To see dots of paint forming now
Chimneys…
Steeple of a church
Modern glass even, among the old perch.

Library Hours

From fourth floor, sitting by the window
The library my resting hour,
To write as a poet,
To dream as if in a sleep
To think, self sitting by that stream
To paint only as an artist
This pretty…pretty picture.
A picture of an old adage
To ease myself of this wordly
Rage,
Each day, to form a new image,
Of my life, so strange,
Quiet…quiet little days.

Sunday Mornings

Sunday mornings
To rise to the whiff of
Luscious breakfast!

Glorious Sunday mornings
Heavenly and beautiful
To hear the little church bells ring.

On Sunday mornings
The church door awaits
Triumphant choir, to awaken
The place.
Smiling pastor stretches his hand
A warm welcome as ever.

For this glory, we stand
In good tether,
To join the singing band.

Sunday school awaits
The little children's pretty plates,
Little sweet cakes pastor's wife
To provide,
While teaching bible stories,
So enlightening,
So bright.

This Clutter

This clutter at times gets to me,
Sheets crumpled,
Pillows scattered,
Clothes strewn about
Video games scattered.
It makes some sense,
This clutter.

They sleep so warm
Covered up close,
Telly still on
Movie on course
Smiles in their sleep
Loved…quite deep.

This clutter every day,
The spill of the coffee
Crumbs from the toast,
Grated cheese left about.
It makes some sense,
This clutter.

We love so warm
Our bond so strong,
That cup of coffee or tea
That slice of toast with cheese.
That glass of milk,
It means so much,
This clutter…it's love.

A Bond

Sparkles and dazzles,
Glitters of gold,
Parties outpoured,
Two pairs of hands.

Beautiful pictures,
Magnificent books,
Lush paintings,
Two pairs of hands.

Wild, spicy dinners,
Ice-cold fizzy drinks,
Ice-cream cake,
Two pairs of hands.

Beautiful adorned clothing,
Well-fitted moccasins.
Video games stashed high,
Two pairs of hands.

Long travelled flight,
On the tropical sight,
Two pairs of hands.

A Life

A life of burden,
A life of sorrows,
Tears, hopes
In vain.

A life of love,
Smiles…cries
Await on fait.

A life of buzz,
A life of tugs,
Hard work…sacrifices
To keep apace.

A life of misuse,
A life of pressures
A life of dreams,
Of love,
Of precious memories.
A life…still yet.

This Child

This child…
Full of life,
Full of joy,
All the laughter in the world
Lots of stuff left untold.

This child,
Is quite naughty,
Boisterous, even haughty!
He chuckles with glee,
I give up, to much plea!

This child,
He cries, he smiles,
Full, of naughty guiles.
Those cheeky ways,
Bless…those endless days.

This child…
Full of stuff,
A whole lot of rough!
Full of love,
He is my little dove!

This Friday

This morning,
Not the same
As many mornings.
Night of torment,
Nightmare and growls,
No sleep.
Crying, I turned to him,
Gentle stroke and a hush,
'my dear, stop the mush.'

This day,
Not like other days,
Stood by the window,
Then I lay on the bed,
Tears…tears…tears…
Uncontrollable,
Racking my body,
Feeling that pain,
Curled up, more tears.
Why?
Why?…why?

This boy,
Not like other boys,
He came to my bed,
Shouting, deeply worried
That his precious mom
Should cry so much,
Feel so much.
'mom, you should not cry.'

The Search

I looked around,
She's nowhere to be found.
Where is she?
I need her to be with me.

I wandered off,
Need something to soothe this cough.
Where is this mother,
I do need a bit of smother!

I went to sleep,
Need someone to pull that sheet.
Where is she?
I do need her to be.

I woke up,
To the smell of that warm pot.
But then, I don't feel at my top.
Will she ever come?
Pray, I do need to have some fun!

Christmas…to Share

Christmas, only months away, yet he has no say
In what to do, no place to go.

This Christmas chime does not seem to be his
To see, among that plan, there is no bliss.

His mittens, they ask for their gifts, their choice
This Christmas, has given him no voice.

Christmas, the warmest time of the year,
Yet it seems hopeless, nothing to cheer.

Christmas for all, no not for some,
Share the joys, the ringing bells, the mistletoe
The gentle peace.
Oh angelic soul, spare him, hand him those keys.

Thoughts of Christmas

I imagine my Christmas, pretty striped candies,
Glowing tree with flashing lights, fluffs of cotton,
Mistletoe, bells, presents, pretty presents.
Ooh! I imagine.

I think of my Christmas,
Warm knitted sweaters, long woolly scarves
Pretty little socks in boots, fluffy hands,
To feel the wondrous snowflakes pouring down,
My arms outstretched to touch.
What a lovely thought!

I need my Christmas,
To sit so warm by that crackling hearth,
Feel the warmth, curled up to hear the
Singing carols,
To stroke my pet, his fur so white, to feel him purr,
In comforted delight.

I see my Christmas,
Family huddled together, smiles and love
Cake and wine to fill our empty stomachs,
Gifts and songs to make the heart merry,
Hugs and kisses to last forever,
Prayers now, to keep us together.

Hampton School

High up in the cold, cold hills,
Through miles of long winding road,
To reach that old bricked gate,
To drive through gravelled paving,
Ferns on both sides.

Old fashioned, in all its grandeur
Built centuries ago, still strong,
In all its allure.
Green, green grass spreading wide and far,
Tennis courts, hockey, volleyball and squash,
Athletics and netball, badminton crash.

The music room, the old mahogany piano plays,
Yet still without one finger to strike the keys
Its melodies to echo, whirring like the breeze.

She strikes a handsome pose, stout and firm,
Shoulders straight, feet together, never untwined.
Her voice booms across the hall, rolling her R's,
Under her tongue, to call the girls loudly,
'no titivating on the corridors!'
to watch her face turned into beechnut red.

Pleasant she was, refined and modest
this old headmistress,
yet she played no games, all her girls well trained
to be dames, language skills her uppermost crust,
perfect speaking, always a must.

Detention, ordermarks, everyday routine,
Naughty behaviour punished, to keep them well gleaned.
Weeding the school garden was one extreme, for all the
Ones refusing to keep the 'cream.'

Nail varnish, jewellery never allowed,
Right coloured socks to fit the crowd,
Sweaters all blue, not one other colour,
Hair combed well neat, shoes well shining,
On perfect pretty feet.

Teachers fat, teachers small
Some grumpy, others pleasant and tall,
English class my absolute favourite,
History too, though boredom never
To reach my face, constant excitement
With my book in place.

Friends were many, bond of love
Us girls together, to strive in one blood,
To share and laugh, with splendid picnics
Out on that matted grass,
Under the shade of the majestic trees,
Holidays near, everything's a cool breeze.

Fair day draws near, visitors to adhere
Old Munroe College, the boys in gear to
Our cheer, to dance in tunes,
'two steps back please,' headmistress speaks,
she constantly watches, poised and pleased.

Munroe College, brother to us,
Same old school, from centuries ago,
Longevity now, a thousand years more,
Just like us, disciplined knowledge,
Old and grey, on porch chair, never to forget
The old, old challenge.

Hampton school, my love for you,
Will be forever, so good to me,
Teachers and friends in my mind as ever.

You've reigned so long,
For many, many years,
Still you are strong, never to fail
You bring my eyes memorable tears.
Long live!
'Summa Virtue Et Humanitate!'

Together

Our two hands entwined
Feeling the warmth
Between our palms
To face each other
Tears of love,
For one another.

Our feet in matching rhythms
Walking slowly
Through the dusky evening
Endearing whispers
From your husky voice,
In my heart
I cry for you.

Our eyes locked together
So much between us to feel
Our lips locked together in
Hungry, fervent passion.

Our love, we cannot deny.

Hearts

You loved me so much
My heart was as soft as a buttercup
My cries for you
Thinking, what should I do?

I tremble with fear
Knowing, you are my true dear.

To hear your voice
So gentle as the breeze
Wooing me over,
With your little tease.

You clasp my hands
Captivate my eyes
My soul,
My being.

To love me so much
For me to love you too
Even for a thousand years,
I will never forget you.

To wilt when you are in sight,
Lose my might
Many a sleepless night…
For me to fight.

Where are you?
I love you too much
I will wait for you…
Please come back for me.

Now,
You are here.
God knows, I have cried
To feel you near,
Your breath on my face.
Truly,
I know,
I will love you,
Always.

Seven-Thirty a.m.

The cool wispy morning
Stepping through the hard white door
Black shining shoes clicking on the floor
Hair blowing through the wind
Bag over shoulder
Case in hand
To walk down the road
To that one bus stand.

The huge oak tree
Branches spreading wide
I look up to see leaves
And saw leaves looking back at me.
I stand alone under this huge tree,
Its outstretched branches,
Like muscled arms,
Protecting me.

The wind blows this quiet morning
Cars pass by, my bus yet…
Still to arrive
My skirt gently blows around my ankles,
Someone else comes to stand,
Stick in hand,
To sit on the bright red stand.

Few more minutes to pass,
Here it comes at last
I show my ticket, to have a seat,
To rest my feet.

My eyes are lustful,
Of beautiful scenery.
And so I watch,
And watch,
And watch.

Moving on the Hill

My life so full of misery
My life, as dark as night
My pain, as hard as iron
My grief, as terrible as death
My friendly nature, gone with the wind
My strength, wilted from suffering.
My love ceases,
No more but a living ghost
Chained,
Muted, bounded.

My ghostly skeleton
Walks through the thin air.

Pitch-black darkness
Surrounds.

Roses once red,
Now black.

Earth once green,
Now dust.

I cry.

Rye on the Hill

Lonely days in my own place
Sadness etched across my face
My mourning and grief dragged
Down to self-disgrace.

Family pictures scattered on fluffy
Beige carpet,
Glowing like a heavenly shrine
In my design
My friends,
All mine.

Clothes strewn from my suitcase
In this cluttered little place.

Books, and more books
Words flying through the air
Pains and emotion
Racking, twisting,
Cries, cries.

I

I love this way,
It pleases me.

I love this read,
It keeps me in good stead.

I love my write,
Keeps me alight.

I love peace,
Not much of a fuss,
Simple, and strong,
Well fitted,
Sparse, but strong.
Love paves the way,
For this,
For that,
For everything.
I love this way.

God's Messenger

Choruses sang in wondrous glory,
Congregation strong, one solid story,
The pastor stands tall, bible in hand
To teach us the good word, keep us in
Good stance.

Sunday school, a pleasurable event,
Children to learn bible stories,
Keep them well learned, of the one supreme,
Who brought them to earth, to enjoy the world?
This heavenly perth.

Pastor at church, friend at home,
Wife alongside, never alone,
To preach the good word, have a pleasant talk,
Keep our family whole,
With that biblical scroll.

Pastor and wife, friends to us,
Pleasant memories never to fade,
One day to rekindle in church,
Those special moments given to us,
Family strong, strong bonded trust.

West at Bay

A palace
In all its grandeur
Guards at gates in black and white
Guns and batons in full sight.

The palace wall,
Delicate intricate design in every
Single block.
Gates wide open to its masterous splendour.

A river in its hypnotising depth
Boats lulling on, perpetual gaze across the bridge
Deep, deep silver glazed water structured across the sky,
Vendors with selling souvenirs
Lovers holding hands
People strolling along above
This precarious deep, deep water.

Over this bridge, no danger to see
Among their buzz, crowd to suntan at its shore
The river sleeps
The river awakes,
Still they buzz around.
The river pulls,
And pulls,
And pulls.

Black Monsters

Group of monsters
Devious ugly ghosts
Satanic in view
As black as nought.

Cruel gruesome monsters
Here they come charging
As vicious as charging chariots
Feet scorched
Walking in scorching heat
For a thousand years,
In groups,
To cause many a fear.

One by one,
From the darkened earth
Stomping, fork in hand
To pitch and carry
An innocent one along,
Full in flesh
Black skeletal beings
Bones as hard as mountains of rocks
Moulded together.
A bone never to crack,
So tough and hard, crusted and baked
These monsters baked together
Ugly in face.

Creatures from hell
Destined for a heavy fell
Chained at feet, for eternity
Loss of sight,
Loss of mind.
No place, no place for them.
No soul…
Itches,
Crawlings,
Bites,
Gnawings,
Rolled in mucky dirt.
I feel sick with disgust,
The scent.

To smell the bounteous garden
Of roses, to appear before me.

Smiling family faces, in every single one
For that beautiful aroma to envelop me,
Some day, some day.

Sheep in the Park

Flocks of sheep
They stride along,
Fleece as pure as snow
Without a shepherd to guide
More like wolves, eyes as red as fire
Ready to tear an innocent lamb,
Sitting by the wayside
To feed on hungry flesh.

Flocks of sheep
Stand on guard
Without any need, only just to stalk
One human, only,
One human without armour
Like hungry lions, they roar,
And roar.

Buried

She lies buried amidst the roses
Underneath that soft earth
Amidst the fields.

Dead so many years
Never to cease, lifelong tears
Her withering soul
Melted into death.

Forever and ever
Gone…
Gone…
Gone.

The cool wind blows softly, so quiet
Ever so quiet
Petals gentle rustle,
She sleeps for eternity
While the world still bustles on
Her children still at grief,
To join someday in relief.

Fruit trees as colourful as a thousand harvests.
The evening in a hushed tone,
At nights, ghostly wails so soft
Meander among the trees, the rivers.

Loved forever
Beneath that soft flowery earth
Dewy,
Dry,
She still lives on…and on.

The Cries of an Indian

For family,
grandmother
grandfather
uncles and aunts
father and mother
sister and cousins too.

Cries,
for the rivers
the livestock
the huge grazing field
the luscious fruit trees
the outstretched lawns.

Cries,
for the smells of the pepper grind
shrimps scalded pink
curled upon that chair
plate in hand,
she appears, hair streaked in white gold,
to please granddaughter.

Long feathery hair rolled in a knot
straight angular nose
small and plump
as gentle as the calming leaves
blowing lightly,
quietly with the wind.

Cries,
for sugary sweets
little gifts here and there.

Cries,
for that little black kitten lying in a basket
covered in blanket,
milk bottle in hand
to gently feed,
to see it suck like a baby
so calm and relaxed
to feel him purr
with delight.

Cries,
for some of the past.

This Old House

Ten rusty windows
old wooden floors, nails sticking through
gruesome-looking wallpaper, several
glued together.
Walls cracked, battered
radiators hanging from the wall
unsightly coloured walls and doors
in dark shades of blue, pink
and orange.

Tank hovers over the toilet,
a little window behind
a bath as old as centuries ago.

A room at the front, as small as a chamber,
a chamber of death
lonely and dark,
only a peep into light.
Shrubs of bushes stand around
other three like living in the forest
yet, it is the city at bay.

Nightfall comes,
stars come out, twinkling in every corner
noises surround, a dog barks
the ice-cream van beepers in
only this makes this place a pleasant sight,
for children
to eat and congregate together, in each other's
houses.

Each day, another misery,
as darkness prevails.
the night watches,
voices sound across the estate
even past the midnight hour,
upstairs and all around
coarse and harsh.

Flowering baskets hang outside,
doors and windows
multitude of colours
dandelions, chrysanthemums, roses
car horns toot in the middle of the day
children run out to play.

bikes, skateboards, lively chatter.

A lonely room…
With one window
One tiny breath of fresh air
Beauteous pictures,
Little bottles of perfume
Books of history
Of romance
The old dictionary
Hats hang on wall, crocheted blouses.

One small elephant in glorious mahogany
its handsome tusks, trumpeting out
the old Indian warrior riding high
on his horse, bow and arrow
headband across forehead
feather in hair, pouch and knife at side,
to envision his horse neighing triumphantly,
the Indian to holler in victory.

The ice-maiden in that soft pose
like a swan on a still pond,
to classical music, she whirls and dances.
The drum, old hard animal skin
to beat a thousand beats,
to echo ten thousand miles,
Like a loud gong sounding
Over and over again.
Bong! Like a gong in a palace.

Hairbrushes, combs
the worn-out shoes
those golden shoes with leoparded sole
sits beside the soft netted slippers
worn with long skirts, to blow with the wind.

Fluffy beige carpet
as soft as feathers
soft under tender feet
bookcase so proud in its place.

One light, to see
into the night
words and words ever to write
words they come,
words they go,
into my head they belong, to keep my sanity, forever and ever along.

The Master

The field lies before me
around the rocky path
beside that little pond,
lilies floating.

Dark and handsome
that striking horse,
his muscled tan
that strong brisk trot,
up and around
black wrought iron gates.

Masterful he sits up high
eyes as glazed as a thousand sunsets
black hat on high
ponytail swishing down backwards
a nose as angular as a sculptor's tool,
clean-shaven, with moustache curved above mouth.

On horse he sits
riding by,
in bushes I hide
to see him once more, my love
for him I will forever adore.

Wayful dreams
of strong master of these mountains and rivers
one lonely maiden, reaching out in hope.

Each day passes by,
they both strut along in their long stride,
each day I hide.

One dusky evening
not far from cottage
our eyes finally meet
to stroke his beautiful creature
to gaze into his eyes.

Master he was
to know I was always there
watching him
every single day.

On horse together we trod
to our mansion.
Only, to love.

Our Wedding Day

One glorious sunny day
from that pretty church
on green, green grass
concreted pavement from gate to door
two doors opened wide.

In the back of the car I arrive,
in a gown as white as snow,
Tiara on head, train of gown trailing behind.
Beautiful bridesmaid walking nearby
Dad on my side, handsomely shaved,
this day, perfectly made.

Family on both sides,
many of them
all willing to see us, wedded to be.

Standing up front, he looks around
handsomely aristocratic, he smiles.
His glazed eyes keeping me in his trance
I smile under my veil, waiting to hold his warm hand,
To feel his warmth,
for him to place that wedding band
On finger,
to tie that knot with his lingering kiss.

This archbishop,
from our church
with bible in hand
to pray for us,
to say our silent vows
'I do.'

Our best man he stands by
smiling for us both
our beautiful bridesmaid
stand beside us, holding bouquet in hand,
In this bond forever made.
To have veil slowly lifted,
to hear our vows,
Our silent warm kiss,
Everyone smiles.

Photograph,
of pretty pictures
hugs and kisses, throughout.

To throw that beautiful bouquet of flowers
so delicately bounteous in my hand
to one lucky person,
as reception awaits on the huge lawns,
of family home, white tables and chairs
a glorious buffet
Wine, lots of wine…
Pretty fruit punches.
Our three tiered wedding cake
with fountain on high, shines out,
magnificently,
Perfectly crafted by master baker.

We sit side by side, as each decided to give a toast,
of knowing us together.
Cameras all set
for him to place that small slice into my mouth,
Us to take a drink from matching wine glasses.

Sister as always, beside to guide me
To be a beautiful hostess on this
Special day, always my friend.
Dad too, without them both it would not do.

Merrymaking, chattering, laughing
Children playing…
Memories still linger on,
our life together
three children now grown, to make us proud.
Thunders, storms
we still live on,
and on
and on,
we love.

Wolverhampton

Visions so vivid in my mind
little blue tricycle, my blue mittens
on small hands
Earmuffs, hat and coat for protect
From wintry weather.

Small wooden gate up front,
to see the milkman
then the soda pop and ice cream
to fill my cheery stomach.

On black gravel I ride,
towards our little playground
with sis.
Snowballs together we make
huge snowman with eyes and ears
as big as magic.

Friends from next door
in swimming pool we play together
beach ball bouncing in the air
swing with seats blow with the wind
on green grass, our holy tether.

The Old Indian Bull

Short with greying hair
His skin as brown as the tree bark
Old grandfather strong and firm as an ox
As he marches through the livestock
Through the wide field,
To leave them grazing on green, green grass
Boots high up to his knees,
He trods around.

Fishnet and hook in hand, then
To head off to rivers to catch
Fish, hundred…and hundreds
To boil under red fiery flame
Bursting from underneath that giant pot.

He sits down on wooden stool
To grind mountains of colourful hot pepper
In that deep wooden mound
Made from tree trunk
Smell of pepper wafting miles away,
Grandpa's nose never to fail
No tears to see
As pepper goes to pot
Blood red shrimps, out they come,
Tied into plastic bags
To sell in markets awide
Rum in hand he drinks
Chattering to gran in native tongue.

Dusk falls,
The stars appear
He sits outside to relax
In the cool wind, with pipe in hand
To sing Indian melodies
Gran beside, grandchild in the middle.

To live his life, with his strong clan,
To work for, to care for,
To die…suddenly.

Huge sepulchre prepared for him
To lay him to rest,
His death to honour.

Feelings

Tears that echo through the wind
Through the storm
Through the rain
Breath of fear that stains
As imminent as death,
Legs that feel twisted and bounded
With chains
Chains that reflect
Moments of anger and envy.

Eyes that cry
As leaves dripping of raindrops
Pelted on cheeks
Its salty taste on tongue
Mingling with saliva
Feelings of outrage.

Lives as those of a cat
To have died and be born again
To feel as though a thousand
Years have passed
In my short life
Bearing the burden of thoughts,
Dreams…changes.

Dreams of a quiet place
far, far away
yearning to fly across the ocean
in reach of a holy land
no one else but me
living among a haze of glowing fields
sunburst flowers
nightfall appears
feathery snowflakes in creative
images dance on the outside
bringing calmness to my lonely soul.
hours as feelings of heaven
as love awaits me beyond.

Seeing wild bushes,
Clumped together, waiting
For blossoming moments
To feel and see the spirit
Of human nature, in unity together.

As we walk
hands clasped together
in a chain filled with
memories
as we walk, as we walk.

Timeless

The years began,
It was a smiling face
Without fear.

The years continued
As the smiling face became sad,
The world had caved in.

Where did all those memories go
All those childish games
Playful ways,
Fairytales as abundance as heaven?

Memories continued,
Child into adulthood
History becomes rife
Literature into drama
Schooldays have droned in.

Sunset rises,
Flowers bloom in abundance
In magical evening
As I stroll on the beach
No more a child as I watch.
The waves gently splash unto
Shore again and again,
As I throw pebble after pebble
Walking barefooted.

Years continue,
Two souls to meet
To create a new life.
A new life
And another…
And another…
Three wholesome lives
To form that ball,
As clear as crystal.

Time has passed,
A chain of fire
In a circle never to depart.
On ships deck
As clouds hover,
The wind to blow around, encircling us.

Raindrops pelt,
As the circle remains steadfast.
A chain of fire
As the time rolls on,
Along with the hourglass.

Chained

My heart begins to ache
Once more
To feel your loving arms
Around me,
No more.
Loneliness grabs me
My eyes begin to swell with tears
His image flashes across my face
And I see him
Knowing only he can fill my place.

His cries I hear, softly thundering
Across the ocean breeze
Through the mountains and the valleys
Yet he never appears
Only in my dreams
He lies.
Buried back within the ocean floors
His need for me, never in reach.

My love,
My love,
My need for you is as great as a
Mountain fire
Unwilling to cease
I need you…
Each day gets more severe
As I feel we will never meet.

My cries can't you hear
My tears can't you feel
Let us make love for all the years.

Yes, I do feel your
Lips on mine
Your firm hands caressing my soul
Your teardrops meeting mine
Our bodies fully untwined.

In our dreams
We remain together
We'll make love
Stormy or sunny weather.

We walk,
Hand in hand
Ghostly fingers gripped
Together.

My darling,
I love you…
I love you…

Prayer

I feel as if the whole world
Has turned down upon me.
They have crushed my spirit.
They have made me feel like
A lowly person.

I feel as my life has been destroyed
That everything has been taken away from me.
I feel as though a dark shadow
Has been placed over me,
As if my life has no purpose.

To have been degraded to such
An extent
To face such humiliation
To ruin my financial freedom
My independence
My life.

No one has ever treated me this way
I wonder when will this ever end,
When will they ever leave me alone?

I have love
I need love
I desire peace
And security,
I need freedom.

Playtime

Birds whistle,
Frogs croak
Wolves howl.

Horses trot
Dogs bark
Cats mew.

Grass moves with the wind
Sun glazes on cobbled path
Reflections of images
In the pond.

White lilies dance
As ghostly faces appear
On tree bark.
Mountains triumph
Sunflowers smile.

A Riddle

Demons gathered together
Colours blended
Standing as wild animals
One as tall as a giraffe,
The other as thin as a gate's spike
Hair as brown as death's dirt
And bald as a drums topping
As wrangled as a gorilla
Looking like just born humans
Grown from the forest.

Wild caged animals bundled
Together, as one stands up as
A yellow bird.
Bellies as huge as sticking beach balls,
Babies pushing babies
Old crows behind computer
Hair scorched with sprays,
One gabbering penguin
Sitting for eternity, distastefully,
Number now 22.

Three they stand
Black, blue and purple
Concocting evilous crime
On innocent needy people
Female, stroking chin as a man's
Beard suddenly appearing, growing down past neck.
One like a nurse,
Standing poised
Still number 22, no answer.

12:00 to the hour, midday now 23,
when will my turn ever come
for my witches free?
The moments tick by
Tick…tock…
Tick…tock…

One as black as an alligator suit
Slithers by,
Two cronies stand twisted
As confused as two blind monkeys
Ten minutes past the hour of the day
Now 30, a witch's view turned away.

And the golden pound of the signgate
Still sits waiting
For the deadly hour
Tick…tock.

Where is the snooping alligator
Slithering all around?
The tall giraffe on his perch
Mouth as a bird, shouting
Like a gong in a wrestling arena.
The cauldron boils
Ring on the left ear
Still the old giraffe stands!

One lonely considering patient
As grieving as the darkest night, hand on chin
Gabbering penguin has disappeared
How weird?
As filthy as a pig in mud
In and then out.
This pig,
He seems a tragedy.
Idiots as usual stroll in
Number 32
Yawn…

Now 36.
The devil's stock
I still wait.
Giraffe appears
Sneers at 12:45 to the hour
At me
A laugh ha! ha!
Black to white
Then white to black
What a creation!

One who stands as a queen
Quite conscious of that glean,
A serpent inside
Growling as a thousand animals.
Strapped up feet appears
Eyes an owl,
To read a strong wrenching verdict.

Now number 48
And beginning to hate
As cauldron boils, and continues to boil.

Match is ready.
Strike one!
A thief has walked in
That really belongs in a rubbish bin.
Time carries on.

Tick…tock.
The disappearing act has occurred.
The thief has gone.

Witches two,
And at the said hour
Now 56
Nine to go
57, near the way to heaven?
Warning!!
Strike two!!
Going, going
Bong!!

Beauty Afflicted

Strolling quietly on the road,
her heart sad,
Life filled of darkness,
As she watches the cars go by
Whispers flowing to her ear,
her whole life wrenched out,
Grabbed away.

The faces are all evil,
Even with the smiles.
Smiles of taunt…and jeers.
she feels like a crushed ball
Rigid to the core,
Afraid, not like before.

That gentle gait of hers,
Long skirt blowing around
her ankles.
Turtleneck blouses…even that,
Could not stop those constant taunts and shouts,
Of perversion.

The cool air blows lightly,
On that pretty face
Lifting that long hair around her.
Feeling lost, and lonely,
The world tumbling down,
Those hands reaching out…
To grab, she ignores

But they never stop.
Are they senile?
Have they no respect?

Her family paints a pretty
Picture in her mind.
She feels softened, yet still lost.
Those ugly demons refuse
To give that rest,
For beauty to live freely,
Without this molest.

They Who

They who sit on high
As time abides by,
Hear no cry,
As babe is left to die.

They who,
Full of power,
Sitting high in their tower,
Hear no plea,
As a crying babe is treated like a flea.

They who,
Drive big cars,
As they put up wars,
Hear no speech
Dictating on one as a leech.

They who,
Are able to give,
Refuse to allow one to live,
To sign a letter,
For life and for better.

They who,
Majestically sit on high
Prey upon you like a dirty fly
Without any purpose for that harsh rewire
They refuse to hear loudening screams,
Of mental anguish,
Left to trod the lonely road without a penny,
To sit at home in a mental cell,
Day in, day out, never well.

They who,
So full of the wicked,
Try to give hateful trick-ed,
Telling you no matter how wise,
Only a disguise may give you that prize.

They who,
live so luxuriantly happy,
they wrestle to keep you down,
To put you into bed, to be welted away like a stupid old nappy.

They who,
Think that they know all,
Never think that one day, they may get a fall,
Pushed against the wall,
To be no more tall, but to be shrivelled like a rottened cabbage,
to be returned…all those years of abusive baggage
on innocent needy people, who they have
left to suffer…in a psychiatric cell.

Dreaming

Blindness occurs during the day
Sight reveals at night as
Everyone has gone astray,
To stand at open window
From up above,
To see out far, way into the forest to
Search for my one and only love.

Hands under chin
With sighs of breath
Feeling that loss so in-depth.

Swans glide so smoothly in pond
As I clutch nightgown around
From cool blustery weather.

In search of stars among the skies
In so much formation
It could not be lies
Only to wonder,
As eyes watch from open window.

Among the moonlight
I see a strong figury sight
Appear from beneath the woods,
My heart skips a ticking beat
Waiting for my love to meet.

He strides towards to me
Straight and firm
Up to my window
To hold my hands.

My eyes still closed, as lips gently
Touch mine
To surrender to charm waited on love
So strong,
I have forgotten how it feels
To be so strong.

My eyes open
As dream fades
My silky hair cascading down,
As I clutch nightgown around,
From cool blustery weather.

True love has gone,
As I close my window.
True love has gone.

Heart with a Voice

That voice I hear in the distance,
Thousand of miles away
Speaking to me day and night
In whispers.

A gentle voice,
In reminder of my past, in livelihood
As I grew under watchful eyes,
To protect.

A familiar voice,
As the years move on
It speaks through thin air,
Thick air,
Snow and storm.
When shall I return?

Should death be my warrant
To unite again in love
In strength
To speak face to face
Of past ventures?

Always that voice,
To bring a tear
As I miss that bond of friendship,
Laughter and tears of happiness.

A voice that whispers.
A voice that worries.
A voice that cries.
A voice that loves.

One Small Dot

Only a small dot
Within the giant world.
A dot, which sinks beneath
The earth,
And rises again, against that giant perth
Which vanishes.

A small dot
Splashed into a thousand pieces
Painting the skies, the seas,
Blown back in one,
As if in fun,
Yet in painful crushes.

One small dot
In murderous pressure
Yet like glittering sparkle
It shimmers,
Splintering,
Leaving annoyance down to a thinner.

If this dot,
Could only remain
As in refined art
Wholesome and sane.

Eternity

It stands eternal every day,
How many more tunes do I have to play on violin so smooth,
Its sweetened chords to keep
It humble and yet aloof?
Expressions of beauty
That tinkle on guitar strings
As the widened sea hums
With its musical links.

Eternal, as piano plays in tune
To its melodious ways.
High notes, low notes
As songs reach out with talented voice,
There's no time for playing about.

Songs of love
Songs of hate
As the jazz band sounds
Slow and melodious, like the blues
Softly, soothing, grabbing woos.

Eternal times to master,
Only the thankful heart
Never to part.
Musical divinity
Lifeline affinity
Only one soul…
Thousands of words.

Earth

Rivers strike, with fire.
Clouds burst, with smoke.
The sun drips, calamity.
Mountains fall, like vanishing ghouls.
Flowers wither, as snake crawls.
The road glides, of fervency.
Oak trees growl, as charging pit bulls.
Lightning bolts, as cracks of whips.
Dust rises as dry moulds of clay
As walking humans
Among the day.

White Gabriels

In hosts they fly across the sky,
Poached and spotted, as the seasons go by.
Wings outspread with glistening claws,
Dripping with blood, from each victim,
As they go across.

Like archangels in glory
They sing in pride
Their bloody murderous plot
To gnaw the brains
Of the gentle,
To cause a clot,
…death to the weak!

In every corner,
In every space,
Stands Gabriel,
A sneer as innocent as a babe,
A laugh as mocking as a rat,
A kiss as poisonous as a snake,
Like a mouthful of cherries
Sweet to the tongue,
Purged to the stomach
Death to the limbs!
Gabriel smiles.

White Gabriels,
Hearts as black as the deepest pit,
Rottened and smelly
Like a thousand dead fish.
White Gabriels,
In a circle they stand as sharpened spears plummet,
Pierced through each brain,
As a torch of fire melts their skin,
Into one mucky mould,
Gummy and buttery,
Whipped and stretched.

It really was in vain.
A new hell has broken.
A little White Gabriel… has reborn.

Happy Moments

Sitting close by the stream,
Eyes locked together, like in a dream.

We play so happy, rubbing noses,
Our bodies enveloped, by beautiful roses.

Our bare feet touch the water,
We splash about, full of laughter.

He stands up strong,
His arms to pull me along.

We run around so carefree
No troubles, we both agree.

Squealing in delight,
On his back I alight.

I feel his arms pull me down,
His face in a false frown.

He pins me to the ground,
His full length having my body, in full bound.

Heavy breathing now,
Our laughs no more.

Our eyes full of tears,
Nevermore, no more fears.

The Edge

Is it the edge of despair,
When I am never able to see my path?

How should I cope when my life is filled
With so much wrath?

Will you tell me how many nights
Of endless sleep should I have,
Before I am able to see my life again?

Must my world feel so daunting,
So dark,
So empty?

There is nothing that you can say,
To calm my soul,
To free my mind,
From this reeling pain,
To live only for nought,
It's all in vain.

The Woes of a Feather

Why was I born
If not to breathe and speak,
Do as I please?

Is not my life my own,
To live as I feel
To do as I think
Without anyone to interfere?

Was I brought into this world
To suffer,
Because of my innocence?
Have you the right to place me
In a psychiatric cell, for you have
Never done well?

Why disgrace my feminine touch,
As barren as a mule I am not
As labour in pain for three, I have not forgot?
Should you not try to be mild,
To calm your senses,
Instead of jumping over vicious fences?

Should you not leave my marital vows alone,
As I grow my life in tightened bond?
My partner is not yours to see or feel.
Were you there when he gave that ring to me?

Why try to disarm me,
A bomb I'm not to detonate?
Should you not have some sleep,
Leave, so I can stop my weep?

You have destroyed my life,
Interfered with me as a wife.
You have caused me severe rife
Sent me to the pigs,
Had you thought I was only here for gold digs?

Revenge

My life has been denied to me,
A situation that has driven me into insanity,
Left to be dragged about like smelly rubbish
Because they cannot compete and gain
Their little fetish.
Bounced about as an animal
Like frogs leaping to and fro
Like kangaroos springing about
And as a blind bird to the slaughter
They…howl about with laughter.

Mirror and powder puffs have disappeared,
Hairbrushes and combs
No more perfumes…
Here I am spinning at my looms
Like a witch dressed in black,
Feet working like magic,
Hoping to create something tragic
While they sit outside and wonder,
If I have gone asunder.

My family has been denied to me
A situation that has taken me into severe calamity,
Left to ponder like a mental baby
Because they would like to see me going crazy,
As the days go by, I become more hazy
While my hair is pulled about,
For all my precious greys to fall out
Which leaves me with a pout.

God knows! Won't they get the hell out?
I mean…go away, have a strong shout.
My interest lies way beyond you.
My family is my love, so get up, find something else to do.

Every day, I spin at the wheel
Hoping to catch just one spider in my web,
So I can torture as I smile.
Thank goodness…here goes,
I have caught the spanking thing,
That has haunted my life,
Ill-treated me off into a mental ring!

Limb my limb,
Nail by nail, fire and blood.

Chants of hell
That one death,
Has made me feel…so well.

Majesty

Life continues,
While I stand still amidst smoke, fire, storm, rainy weather
Sleet and snow,
My image appearing through tall golden sheaves
Transforming into old oak trees,
Water rising and falling, slow-moving rhythm,
As I begin to transform.

Death awaits,
As the sun opens wide
The grass becomes green
Flowers bloom
Children play
Around a castle made only for peace.

Times have come and gone
As we move with the tide
Whether slow or fast.
The pole of life stands, wrapped like a ribbon
Painted as on canvas
As snakes slither along dusty ground
Fern trees swaying to and fro
We remain quiet,
We smile
We sigh.

Changes

Flowers bloom,
Grass grow
Mountains divide
Animals surround,
My side.

Rains fall,
Butterflies flutter
Honeysuckles wither
From swarm of bees
To their teas.
Wintertime,
All forestry glory in quiet mime.
Sleep as the naked branches
To await the snow
In quiet bow.
Now my lights are out,
To sleep.

The Near End

The heavens have fallen,
The skies have closed
The sun vanished.
Now,
The moon has sunk
Into the open earth,
The stars in a box
Closed magically tight,
The mountains as flat
As folded blankets.
The grass like woven thread,
The stones in one molten boulder.
'Tis now closed.
Life has ceased.

Beauty of the Bamboo

Miles and miles of bamboo
Overlapping above,
Hailing so majestic
For everyone giving love.

Green green bamboo
Beauteous sight to see,
Above straight paved road
As buses and cars drive,
It suddenly becomes alive.

Cool wispy evening
Plantations domain
Mystical silence
As bamboos hover.
In protection it appears,
A God made creation
To last for all the years.

Like clasped hands
Friendship stands,
With overlapping bamboos,
Leading us to the seas, the ships,
Fishermen grips.

Miles and miles of bamboo.

Unison

Cards on the table,
In a round circle
On a round table,
Only six people.

Six,
Old and grey
A deck in each hand
Cigar in mouth,
Wavering for one single magical wand, to give a stand.

One lighted lantern
In a dark room
Hung above high,
To send off shadows
From widened eyes.

Faces growl
Upon old cronies.
Ghostly faces hidden in the walls,
To see snickering grins,
Card in shoe
Cheating wrinkly hands
Beer bursting from buckled waistbands.

Midnight,
Cards still ashuffle
Drunken slurs
Rain downpours
Lightning flashes,
Low throaty laughs,
It has been a long awaited win.

Triumphant they stand,
Beer in hand
As they give a thank,
For prosperous prank.

Shadows sway
Under lighted lamps
While ghostly faces watch.
In line they stride,
With shoeless pride,
The rain continues to pour, lights bolt across the sky. Flash!

Printed in the United States
24693LVS00001B/223-228

9 781413 743418